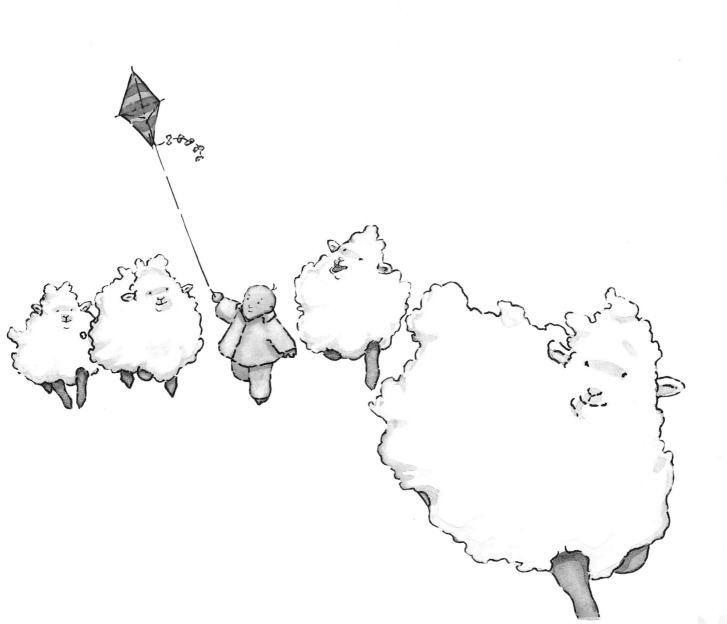

Counting SHEEP.

Barbara McGee

Annick Press Ltd., Toronto, Canada

Second printing, July 1991

Annick Press gratefully acknowledges the support of
The Canada Council and the Ontario Arts Council.

Canadian Cataloguing in Publication Data

McGee, Barbara, 1961 –
    Counting Sheep

ISBN 1-55037-157-6 (bound). – ISBN 1-55037-160-6 (pbk)

I. Title.

PS8575.G4C6 1991   jC813'.54   C90-095316-0
PZ7.M34Co 1991

Distributed in Canada and the U.S.A. by:
Firefly Books Ltd.,
250 Sparks Avenue
North York, Ontario
M2H 2S4

The art in this book was rendered in watercolour.
The text has been set in Stone Informal.

Printed and bound in Canada
by D. W. Friesen & Sons.
Printed on acid free paper ∞

Edward's Grandma once told him that she counted sheep to fall asleep.

One night Edward was counting sheep
(very quietly so he wouldn't wake his cat).

He wasn't expecting company.

He didn't want to
be rude, but he
wasn't sure he
should let them all in.

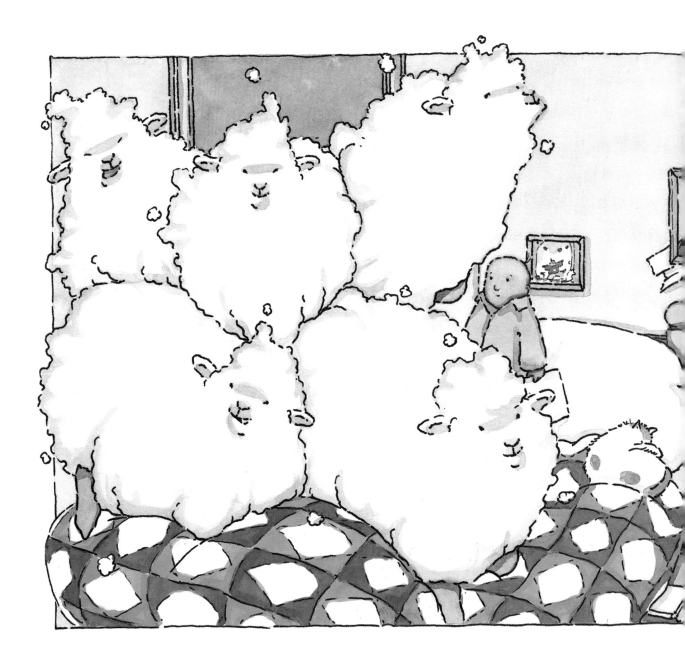

They invited themselves in
...with some difficulty
(and without waking his cat).

Although they couldn't read,
they found Edward's counting book

...very interesting.

They invited him out...

to play

and play

and play.

They played
very happily
together.

When they stopped to admire the moon

Edward yawned.

So they all went home

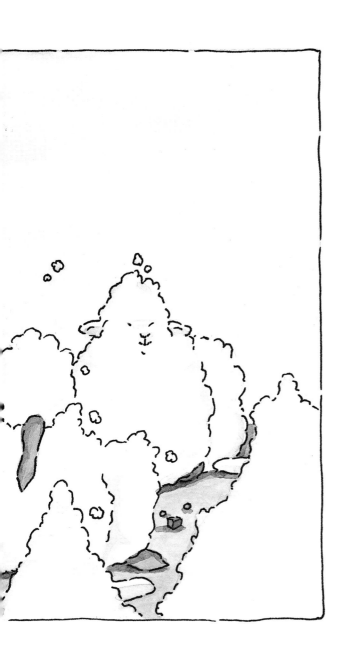

to bed.

Edward would have to ask
Grandma what sheep
eat for breakfast.

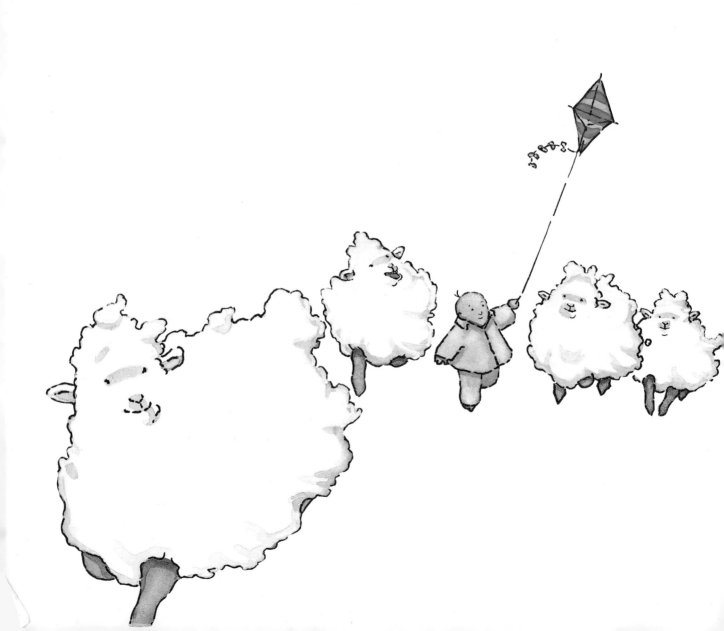